From Matthew
Kawamoto #9

A JAPANESE FOLKTALE

A TALE OF TWO TENGU

Retold by
Karen Kawamoto McCoy

Illustrated by
Koen Fossey

ALBERT WHITMAN & COMPANY • MORTON GROVE, ILLINOIS

Text typeface: Trump Mediaeval.
Illustration media: Pen and acrylic paint.
Designer: Karen Johnson Campbell.

Library of Congress Cataloging-in-Publication Data
McCoy, Karen Kawamoto.
A tale of two tengu/Karen Kawamoto McCoy;
illustrated by Koen Fossey.
p.   cm.
Summary: Two Japanese goblins with long, lovely noses
decide to prove once and for all whose proboscis is the
more wonderful.
ISBN 0-8075-7748-0
[1. Fairy tales. 2. Folklore—Japan. 3. Goblins—Folklore.]
I. Fossey, Koen, ill. II. Title.
PZ8.M4575Tal 1993   93-2
398.21—dc20   CIP
[E]   AC

For Ed and Kevin, with all my love. KKM
To Kobie and Wietse, my two quarreling goblins. KF

Tengu are Japanese goblins with long,
lovely noses. Once there were two such creatures, one blue
and one red, living in the high mountains of Japan.

Kenji and Joji were proud of their extraordinary noses.
Like powerful springs, these noses could be stretched out
for miles and then snapped back to their original size. The
two tengu were always fighting because each believed his
nose was the more wonderful.

One day a delicious odor tickled Kenji's nose. "What smells so good?" the blue tengu wondered, peering down his mountain. He decided to follow the fragrant smell with his nose. WHOOSH! Kenji's nose grew long, long, longer.

Soon it looked more like a skinny blue pole than a nose. The wobbling pole skimmed over seven mountaintops and flopped across prickly plains. Finally it stopped on the terrace of Lord Nakamura's mansion.

Inside the mansion, a great party was going on. Princess Fumiko had invited all her friends, princesses from far and near. They were taking turns lifting beautiful kimonos from her treasure chest. Pouches of fragrant spices had been layered between the kimonos. And that's what had tickled Kenji's nose.

Princess Fumiko was just holding up a pretty pink kimono when she spotted Kenji's nose. "What's this?" she said. She stepped outside and examined the skinny pole. "Let's hang the kimonos here!" the princess called to her maids. The maids hung the beautiful pieces of material on the long blue pole.

Meanwhile, Kenji felt a strange itching sensation. But his arms were too short to scratch the troublesome itch! So he snapped his long nose back towards the mountain.

WHOOSH! The blue pole shrank short, short, shorter. "What's happening to our pole?" the princesses shouted, trying to catch the flying kimonos. But the skinny blue pole disappeared as quickly as it had appeared.

"Amazing!" exclaimed Kenji, as the bright array
of material swished into view. He was so pleased that
he forgot all about scratching himself. He marched around,
being careful not to drag any of the beautiful kimonos on
the ground.

Later that same afternoon, Kenji hiked over to the next mountain to visit Joji.

"See my beautiful nose!" Kenji cried. He pranced around the red tengu. The rainbow-colored kimonos fluttered in Joji's face.

"That's nothing!" Joji said angrily, turning an even deeper red. "Just watch what *my* nose brings back!"

    For the next seven days, Joji sat on his mountain, hoping some delicious odor would come to him. But nothing happened. Finally he grew impatient. "I can't wait any longer," he complained. "I'll let my nose find something good."

    WHOOSH! Joji's nose grew long, long, longer. Soon it looked more like a skinny red pole than a nose. The long red pole skimmed the tops of the seven mountains and bobbed over the prickly plains.

Finally it stopped in Lord Nakamura's garden.
Prince Isao and his friends were chasing each other
through the lush greenery. When the prince saw
Joji's nose, he cried, "Look at the terrific red pole!"

The boys raced to the pole and climbed aboard. They took turns thumping and jumping on it. Then Prince Isao found a piece of rope and fashioned a swing. The boys swung higher and higher.

Back on his mountain, Joji could feel the pounding on his poor nose. "Ouch!" he screamed every time a boy stomped on him. His nose felt so heavy he thought he could barely move it. Never had it hurt so much!

The screams brought Kenji rushing to Joji's mountain. "Are you hurt?" he asked.

"No!" Joji answered angrily. He snapped his nose back towards the mountain.

WHOOSH! The red pole shrank short, short, shorter. "What's happening to our pole?" the boys shouted as they toppled into the plants.

"Aaah," Joji sighed, as the end of his nose came into view. Now it was twice as red as normal and swollen from all the pounding.

The sight was so funny that Kenji just had to laugh. "Tomorrow at sunrise," said Joji angrily, "we *both* send our noses down into the plains."

"Haven't you had enough?" Kenji asked between chuckles.

Joji shook his head. "We'll just see who snares the best prize!" he shouted. He jumped up and strutted away.

Early the next day, as the first rays of sun lit the morning sky, the two tengu met on Joji's mountaintop. At the count of five, both Kenji and Joji released their noses. WHOOSH! The two noses grew long, long, longer. Soon two skinny poles, one red and one blue, raced over the seven mountains and flopped across the prickly plains.

Once again the long, skinny poles reached Lord Nakamura's mansion. Moments before, a servant had raised the bamboo blinds to let in the warm rays of sunshine. Kenji's nose zipped in one window. Joji's nose whizzed in another window.

The Nakamuras were sitting down to breakfast. A fine meal of bean jam buns and steaming rice tea stood on the table. But no one noticed the breakfast. Two long, bobbing poles had just wobbled into the room!

"Look," cried Princess Fumiko. "That's the blue pole that stole my kimonos!"

"And that's the red pole that threw me down in the garden!" yelled Prince Isao.

"Guards, seize those poles!" ordered Lord Nakamura.

The guards rushed in. When they tugged on the poles, the silly noses grew all the longer. They tried winding the poles up into coils. But the coils sprang out, knocking down the poor guards.

Princess Fumiko tugged on her father's sleeve. "I know what to do," she said. "Let's tie the poles into a giant knot so they won't get away."

The guards approached the unruly poles. Some grabbed the skinny red nose and some picked up the skinny blue nose. Struggling, they wove the two poles back and forth into one gigantic knot.

Back on the mountain, the tengu could feel the twisting and tugging on their noses.

"Look at my nose jiggle!" exclaimed Joji. "I must have a ton of treasure on it!"

"My nose feels strange too!" cried Kenji. "I wonder—"

"Not as strange as mine!" interrupted Joji. "I bet I have *two* tons of treasure."

"Why don't we find out?" Kenji challenged Joji.

At the count of five, the tengu started retrieving their long noses. WHOO—WHOOSH! But something weird was happening! Instead of their noses snapping back to them, Kenji and Joji found themselves being hurtled forward.

First they tumbled down the steep mountainside.
Then they whizzed over the seven mountains, skimming
the jagged tops of a few. Next came the prickly plains and
then the walls of Lord Nakamura's mansion.

The tengu screeched to a stop, just inches from the
mansion. They felt pierced and torn from all the jostling.
Dazed, they rested against the wall. Then they climbed up
and peered in the windows.

The tengu watched as Lord Nakamura and his wife
and children ate their breakfast. Then everyone left
the room, and Joji and Kenji crawled in through the
windows.

"What's this?" said the tengu. They stared at the huge
red-and-blue knot.

Joji pulled impatiently on his nose. The knot grew
tighter.

"Stop!" Kenji cried. "Tugging only makes it worse!"

Joji started moaning. "This is what I get for being so jealous of you!"

"Quit complaining," scolded Kenji. "We must work together to free our noses. You rest," he said, "and I'll try first."

The tengu took turns, resting and working until, loop by loop, tangle by tangle, the monstrous knot was slowly unraveled. At last two skinny noses drooped free in the center of the room. "Aaah!" the tengu sighed, rubbing their aching noses.

Suddenly Lord Nakamura strode into the room. "Tengu?" he said, his eyes growing as round as teacups. "So the skinny poles belong to you!" He eased one hand out of his kimono sleeve and cautiously reached for the long blue nose.

Kenji backed away from the burly hand. He tugged on Joji's arm. "Let's go!" he said.

The tengu dove out the nearest window, their noses trailing behind them.

They hurtled the mansion wall, sped across the prickly plains, and clambered over the seven mountains. They didn't stop until they came to Joji's mountain. Only then did they snap in their noses. WHOOSH! The silly things grew short, short, shorter.

Joji collapsed. "That is the last time I ever send my nose away from home!"

"Me, too!" sighed Kenji, plopping down. "It's so painful!"

After a few minutes, Kenji struggled to a stand. "From now on, we work together!" He bowed his deepest bow.

"Good idea!" Joji rose slowly and bowed back. Smiles flashed across the two faces.

Since that day, Kenji and Joji have been the best of friends. Never again have they argued about whose nose is more wonderful—well, *almost* never!